小鼠拍檔
康柏與小波
cornbread & poppy

馬修‧科戴爾 Matthew Cordell ／文圖

劉清彥／譯

三民書局

獻給茱莉——

我是康柏，妳是我的小波。

小書芽

小鼠拍檔：康柏與小波

文　　圖	馬修‧科戴爾
譯　　者	劉清彥
責任編輯	江奕萱

發 行 人	劉仲傑
出 版 者	弘雅三民圖書股份有限公司
地　　址	臺北市復興北路 386 號 (復門門市)
	臺北市重慶南路一段 61 號 (重南門市)
電　　話	(02)25006600
網　　址	三民網路書店 https://www.sanmin.com.tw

出版日期	初版一刷 2023 年 5 月
書籍編號	H859980
Ｉ Ｓ Ｂ Ｎ	978-626-307-979-3

弘雅三民圖書

❄ 目錄 ❄

❄ 第一場雪 ❄

冬天到了。第一片雪花飄落下來。

康柏待在家裡，整理、保存收成
季節採集的水果、穀物和起司。

扭緊！

每年秋天，康柏都會擔心自己沒有足夠的食物度過冬天。

不過，他也很喜歡做計畫和準備。

畢竟，要度過漫長又寒冷的冬天，需要有妥善的規畫才行。

6

康柏最好的朋友小波，
卻一點都不擔心。

8

她ㄊㄚ熱ㄖㄜˋ愛ㄞˋ冒ㄇㄠˋ險ㄒㄧㄢˇ，
也ㄧㄝˇ喜ㄒㄧˇ歡ㄏㄨㄢ騎ㄑㄧˊ腳ㄐㄧㄠˇ踏ㄊㄚˋ車ㄔㄜ。

9

她_{ㄊㄚ}熱_{ㄖㄜˋ}愛_{ㄞˋ}健_{ㄐㄧㄢˋ}行_{ㄒㄧㄥˊ}，也_{ㄧㄝˇ}喜_{ㄒㄧˇ}歡_{ㄏㄨㄢ}和_{ㄏㄜˊ}康_{ㄎㄤ}柏_{ㄅㄛˊ}在_{ㄗㄞˋ}她_{ㄊㄚ}家_{ㄐㄧㄚ}盪_{ㄉㄤˋ}鞦_{ㄑㄧㄡ}韆_{ㄑㄧㄢ}。

10

只ㄓ是ㄕ，她ㄊㄚ不ㄅㄨ喜ㄒㄧ歡ㄏㄨㄢ做ㄗㄨㄛ計ㄐㄧ畫ㄏㄨㄚ和ㄏㄜ準ㄓㄨㄣ備ㄅㄟ，
也ㄧㄝ不ㄅㄨ喜ㄒㄧ歡ㄏㄨㄢ採ㄘㄞ集ㄐㄧ食ㄕ物ㄨ。

她ㄊㄚ總ㄗㄨㄥ是ㄕ拖ㄊㄨㄛ到ㄉㄠ最ㄗㄨㄟ後ㄏㄡ一ㄧ刻ㄎㄜ才ㄘㄞ做ㄗㄨㄛ，幾ㄐㄧ乎ㄏㄨ
找ㄓㄠ不ㄅㄨ到ㄉㄠ什ㄕ麼ㄇㄜ食ㄕ物ㄨ了ㄌㄜ。

「砰ㄆㄥ！砰ㄆㄥ！」康ㄎㄤ柏ㄅㄛ家ㄐㄧㄚ門ㄇㄣ外ㄨㄞ傳ㄔㄨㄢ來ㄌㄞ敲ㄑㄧㄠ
門ㄇㄣ聲ㄕㄥ。

「該去採集過冬的食物了！」小波大叫。

「小波！」康柏說。「冬天已經到了啊！妳還沒有準備好食物嗎？現在早就都沒有了！」

「『都沒有了』是什麼意思啊？」

「妳不記得我有找妳一起去山姆的牧場搬起司嗎？」康柏問。

「我說『他快賣完了。』結果妳回答什麼？」

「那時我正在騎腳踏車啊！」小波說。

「妳不記得我要幫妳去豪斯費勒的田裡收集穀物嗎？」康柏問。

「我說『穀物剩下不多了。』結果妳回答什麼？」

「不要，我晚點再去，」小波說。

「可是我那天要去健行啊！」

「妳不記得我叫妳去溫克奶奶的農場採莓果嗎？」康柏問。

「我說『莓果快要沒有了。』結果妳回答什麼？」

「不要，我晚點再去，」小波說。
「那時我正在盪鞦韆啊！」

19

冬天裡沒有食物是一件危險的事。

「喔，糟糕，康柏！」小波說。
「喔，糟糕，小波！」康柏說。

「來吧，小波，我們到處問問
看，還有沒有剩下的食物。」

山姆的起司
沒了。

豪斯費勒的穀
物也沒了。

溫克奶奶的莓果也都沒了。
「說不定，」小波說，「有鄰居
還有多的食物。」

「下次請早！」鎮上最壞脾氣的老賴瑞說。

「現在該怎麼辦？」康柏問。他
不能讓自己最好的朋友挨餓。
「我分一些食物給妳吧。」

「可是，這樣你就沒有辦法撐過
整個冬天了……」小波說。「我
不知道該怎麼辦。」

小波看著窗外，視線掃過整個小鎮，再越過山谷，所有的食物都被採集完了。接著，她看向遠處那座山。

「也許……吼吼山上還有食物。」小波說。

呼ㄏ 呼ㄏ 山？！

「沒ㄇㄟˊ有ㄧㄡˇ老ㄌㄠˇ鼠ㄕㄨˇ會ㄏㄨㄟˋ去ㄑㄩˋ吼ㄏㄡˇ吼ㄏㄡˇ山ㄕㄢ耶ㄧㄝˊ！」康ㄎㄤ
柏ㄅㄛˊ尖ㄐㄧㄢ叫ㄐㄧㄠˋ。

的ㄉㄜˊ確ㄑㄩㄝˋ，大ㄉㄚˋ家ㄐㄧㄚ都ㄉㄡ不ㄅㄨˋ敢ㄍㄢˇ上ㄕㄤˋ吼ㄏㄡˇ吼ㄏㄡˇ山ㄕㄢ。

他們一起望向窗外，然後仰頭看著那座山。

忍不住發抖起來。

27

❄ 吼吼山 ❄

「吼吼山的岩石又陡又滑，妳可能會跌倒！」康柏說。

「我知道。」小波說。

28

「吼吼山有貓頭鷹！貓頭鷹最愛吃老鼠！」

「我知道。」小波說。

「露西小姐上吼吼山採集食物後，就再也沒有回來了！」

「我知道。」小波說。

那真是一件令人難過的事。露西小姐是唯一一隻敢登上吼吼山的老鼠。那已經是幾年前的事了。從那以後，就再也沒有誰見過她、聽過她的消息，也再也沒有老鼠敢上吼吼山了。

露西小姐

「這是唯一的方法。」小波說。

「唯一的方法？」康柏問。他很擔心，而且他不像小波那麼愛冒險。但小波是他最好的朋友，他不能讓小波自己去。「那我跟妳一起去。」

33

他們把採集食物的工具放在小波的拖車上。

然後穿上外套，戴好帽子，圍上圍巾。他們開始爬山。

爬呀、爬呀，他們一步步往上爬。到目前為止，一切順利。沒有遇到貓頭鷹，可是也沒有發現任何食物。而且雪越下越大。

「那是黑莓叢嗎？」小波問。

奇怪，所有的黑莓都被摘光了。

38

他們繼續爬山，雪不停的下著。

「那些是玉米稈嗎？」康柏問。
可是玉米也都沒了。

他們繼續爬山，積雪越來越深，
他們也越爬越辛苦。

「那是小麥嗎？」小波問。

就ㄐㄧㄡˋ在ㄗㄞˋ那ㄋㄚˋ時ㄕˊ，有ㄧㄡˇ個ㄍㄜ大ㄉㄚˋ大ㄉㄚˋ的ㄉㄜ影ㄧㄥˇ子ㄗˇ飛ㄈㄟ過ㄍㄨㄛˋ他ㄊㄚ們ㄇㄣ的ㄉㄜ路ㄌㄨˋ徑ㄐㄧㄥˋ上ㄕㄤˋ方ㄈㄤ，他ㄊㄚ們ㄇㄣ仰ㄧㄤˇ起ㄑㄧˇ頭ㄊㄡˊ。

41

「貓頭鷹！」他們大聲尖叫。

他們丟下拖車，跑向最近的
灌木叢。

43

周圍的雪地傳來唰 …… 唰 …… 唰
的聲音。貓頭鷹已經著地了。

嗅ㄒㄧㄡˋ⋯⋯嗅ㄒㄧㄡˋ⋯⋯「這ㄓㄜˋ是ㄕˋ老ㄌㄠˇ鼠ㄕㄨˇ的ㄉㄜ˙味ㄨㄟˋ道ㄉㄠˋ嗎ㄇㄚ˙？」有ㄧㄡˇ個ㄍㄜˋ聲ㄕㄥ音ㄧㄣ說ㄕㄨㄛ。

康ㄎㄤ柏ㄅㄛˊ和ㄏㄜˊ小ㄒㄧㄠˇ波ㄅㄛ抖ㄉㄡˇ得ㄉㄜ˙好ㄏㄠˇ厲ㄌㄧˋ害ㄏㄞˋ，連ㄌㄧㄢˊ灌ㄍㄨㄢˋ木ㄇㄨˋ叢ㄘㄨㄥˊ也ㄧㄝˇ跟ㄍㄣ著ㄓㄜ˙顫ㄓㄢˋ抖ㄉㄡˇ。

「我喜歡老鼠！」那個聲音說。

灌木叢沙沙沙的抖著。

小波抓起一顆石頭，站了起來。

「我掩護你，康柏！快跑！」

她ㄊㄚ用ㄩㄥ石ㄕ頭ㄊㄡ丟ㄉㄧㄡ中ㄓㄨㄥ了ㄌㄜ貓ㄇㄠ頭ㄊㄡ鷹ㄧㄥ的ㄉㄜ爪ㄓㄨㄚ子ㄗ。

48

「喔！妳為什麼用石頭丟我？」貓頭鷹大叫。「我喜歡老鼠。老鼠是我的朋友耶。」

「我們……我們以為貓頭鷹喜歡吃老鼠？」小波說。

「我不是，」貓頭鷹說。「我吃素啦。」

這隻巨大蓬鬆又頻頻抽鼻子的貓頭鷹，高高的站在他們面前。

「我叫伯納。」他說。

「抱歉，伯納……我叫康柏。」

「抱歉，伯納……我叫小波。」

「你們在山裡做什麼啊？」伯納問。「我很少在山上這裡看到老鼠耶。」

「我們在找食物。」康柏說。

「我知道一個有食物的地方。而且還很多喔！」伯納說。

康柏和小波聽了好開心。

「可以帶我們去嗎？」小波一邊問，一邊整理自己的拖車。

「當然可以！如果你們跳上來，就能更快到了！」伯納願意載他們去。

於是他們就飛上了天。

❄ 食物危機 ❄

過了一會兒，他們降落在一棟小木屋前。小木屋的煙囪飄出了裊裊炊煙。

喀一啦……

「這是我朋友家！」伯納說。

小木屋的門緩緩推開，有隻上了年紀的老鼠出來迎接他們。

「露ㄌㄨˋ西ㄒㄧ小ㄒㄧㄠˇ姐ㄐㄧㄝˇ！你ㄋㄧˇ（你ㄋㄧˇ們ㄇㄣ˙）認ㄖㄣˋ識ㄕˋ露ㄌㄨˋ西ㄒㄧ小ㄒㄧㄠˇ姐ㄐㄧㄝˇ？」伯ㄅㄛˊ納ㄋㄚˋ、康ㄎㄤ柏ㄅㄛˊ和ㄏㄢˊ小ㄒㄧㄠˇ波ㄅㄛ異ㄧˋ口ㄎㄡˇ同ㄊㄨㄥˊ聲ㄕㄥ的ㄉㄜ˙說ㄕㄨㄛ。

「康柏！小波！天啊，真是好久不見了！」露西小姐說。「快進來取暖！」

「再見了，朋友們！」伯納拍拍他的大翅膀，升空離開，飛進吼吼山。

「露西小姐，我們還以為妳……失蹤了。」康柏說。

「我是失蹤了，好吧，我只是離開原本的環境，搬到山上來住。我喜歡自己生活！」露西小姐說。「不過，我很高興終於有老鼠朋友來陪我！你們為什麼會來這裡呢？」

他們向露西小姐解釋了小波的食物危機。

「伯納認為妳有一些食物可以分享給我們？」小波害羞的問。

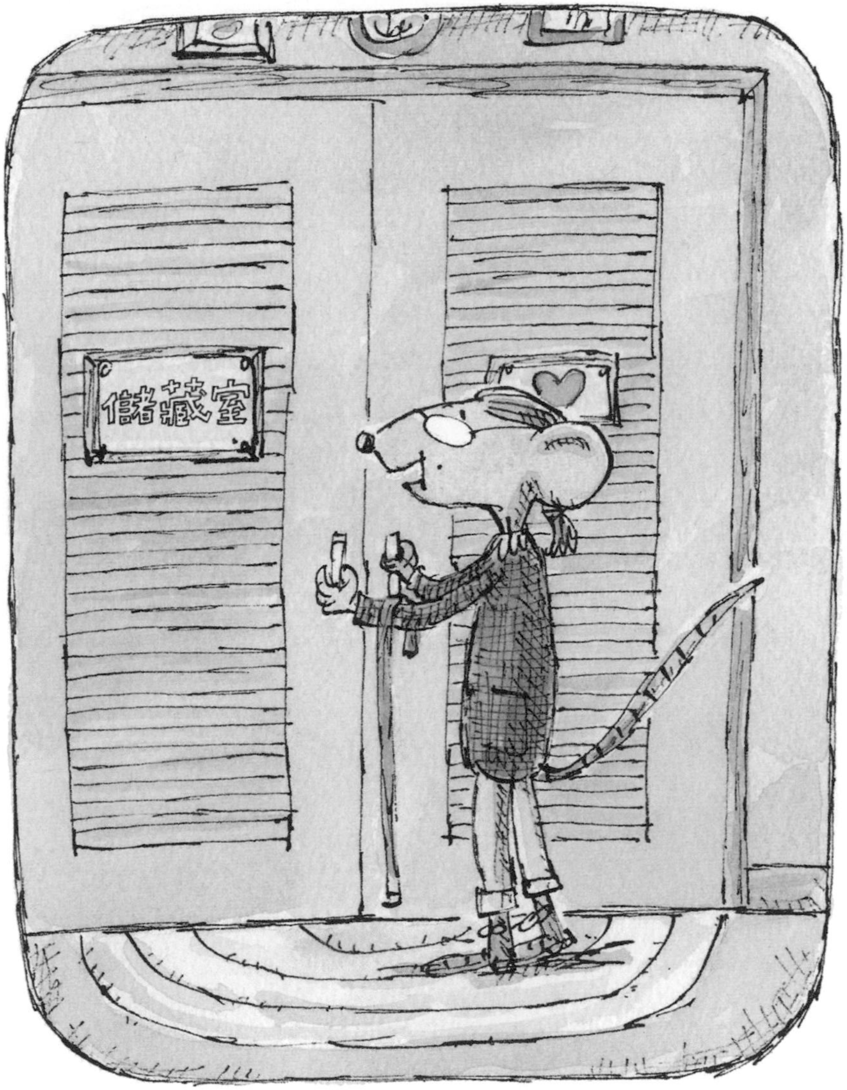

「喔，有啊！」露西小姐說。

「我儲存好幾年了！我是吼吼山上唯一一隻採集和儲存食物的老鼠。想拿什麼儘管拿吧！」

到處都是一罐罐保存好的莓果。

還有一袋袋穀物，和一大塊一大
塊起司。

「可是在你們離開前，一定要喝
一杯露西小姐特調的茶！」他們
的朋友說。

時候不早了，露西小姐幫他們打包好食物，甚至還送了一罐自己特製的茶葉。

然後為他們在腳上和拖車上都扣緊滑雪板，可以加快他們回家的速度。

「非常謝謝妳，露西小姐！」小波說。「妳真是我的救命恩人！我該怎麼報答妳呢？」

「偶爾回來看看我就行了！」露西小姐說。

康柏和小波踩著
滑雪板，快速滑
下山。

小波當然愛死了。

康柏覺得很驚訝，
他居然也喜歡滑雪。

真ㄓㄣ是ㄕ一一趟ㄊㄤ有ㄧㄡ趣ㄑㄩ的ㄉㄜ冒ㄇㄠ險ㄒㄧㄢ。

到了小波家，他們把所有食物一
一卸下、擺好。

雪積得好深，康柏還幫忙小波剷
出一條通道。

他們喝了一杯露西小姐的茶，犒賞自己完成一件了不起的事。

「敬老朋友。」小波說。

「我們再來滑雪吧！」康柏說。

「康柏，我們不是應該去你家剷
雪嗎？天色快暗了。」

「不ㄅㄨ要ㄧㄠ，我ㄨㄛ晚ㄨㄢ點ㄉㄧㄢ再ㄗㄞ去ㄑㄩ！」康ㄎㄤ柏ㄅㄛ回ㄏㄨㄟ答ㄉㄚ。

cornbread & poppy

matthew cordell

To Julie—
the Poppy to my Cornbread

❄ Contents ❄

❄ The First Snow ❄

It was winter. The first snowflake had
fallen.

Cornbread was home, putting away all
he had foraged from harvest time: fruit
preserves, grains, and cheeses.

Every autumn,
Cornbread worried
he would not have
enough food to get
through winter.

But he also loved to
plan and prepare.

It took a lot of
planning to get
through those long,
cold winter months.

6

Cornbread's best friend, Poppy,
was not one to worry.

She loved adventure.

She loved to ride bikes.

9

She loved to take hikes. And she loved to
play on the swing set with Cornbread at
her house.

But she did not love to plan or prepare.
She did not love to forage.

She always put it off till the very last
minute. And she was almost out of food.

BOOM! BOOM! There was a knock at
Cornbread's door.

"Time to forage for winter!" yelled Poppy.

"Poppy!" said Cornbread, "It *is* winter! You didn't get your food? Surely, it's all gone by now!"

"What do you mean, 'all gone'?"

"Don't you remember," asked Cornbread, "when I asked you to come with me to get your cheese from Sam's Dairy?

"'He's almost out,' I said. And what did you say?"

"But I was riding my
bike!" Poppy said.

"Don't you remember," asked Cornbread, "when I offered to help you get your grains from Horsefeather's fields? 'There's not much left,' I said. And what did you say?"

"'Nah, I'll do it later,'" Poppy said. "But I was going hiking that day!"

"Don't you remember," asked Cornbread, "when I told you to pick your berries from Grandma Winkle's farm? 'They're almost gone,' I said. And what did you say?"

"'Nah, I'll do it later,'" Poppy said. "But I was playing on my swing set!"

A winter without food is a dangerous thing.

"Oh no, Cornbread!" said Poppy.

"Oh no, Poppy!" said Cornbread.

"Come on, Poppy, let's ask around and see if there's any food left."

Sam was
out of cheese.

Horsefeather was
out of grains.

Grandma Winkle was all out of berries.

"Maybe," said Poppy, "one of the neighbors
has extra."

"Shouldn't have waited so long!" said
Old Larry, the town grump.

SLAM!
NOPE

"What now?" asked Cornbread. He couldn't let his best friend go hungry. "I'll give you some of my food."

"But then you won't have enough to last the winter...," said Poppy. "I don't know what to do."

Poppy looked out the window. She looked
out over the town and past the valley, where
all the food had already been foraged. Then
she looked up at the mountain.

"There might be food...on Holler Mountain,"
said Poppy.

"No one goes up Holler Mountain!"
shrieked Cornbread.

It was true. No one dared go up Holler
Mountain.

They both look out the window, then up at the mountain.

And they shivered.

❄ Holler Mountain ❄

"There are steep, slippery rocks on Holler Mountain. You could fall!" said Cornbread.

"I know," said Poppy.

"There are owls on Holler Mountain!
Owls eat mice!"

"I know," said Poppy.

"Ms. Ruthie went up Holler Mountain to forage for food. She never came back!"

"I know," said Poppy.

It was a sad story. Ms. Ruthie was the only mouse to ever dare go up Holler Mountain. It was years ago, and she was never seen or heard from since. No one ever went up the mountain again.

"It's the only way," said Poppy.

"The only way?" asked Cornbread. Cornbread was worried. And he didn't love adventure like Poppy did. But Poppy was his best friend. And he could not let her go alone. "Then I'm coming with you."

They collected Poppy's wagon and harvesting supplies.

They bundled up in scarves, hats, and jackets. They began their climb up the mountain.

36

Up, up, up the mountain they went. And so far, so good. There were no owls. But they hadn't found any food yet either. And a heavier snow had now begun to fall.

"Are those blackberry bushes?" Poppy asked.

Strangely, all the berries had been picked.

Up the mountain they went. The snow continued to fall.

"Are those cornstalks?" asked Cornbread. The corn was all gone too.

Up the mountain they went. The snow was getting deeper, and it was getting harder and harder to climb.

"Is that wheat up there?" asked Poppy.

Just then, a large shadow flew over their path. They looked up.

"An owl!" they screamed.

They dropped the wagon and ran for the
nearest shrub.

The snow crunch…crunch…crunch…
crunched around them. The owl had
landed.

Sniff…sniff… "Is that mice I smell?" said a voice.

Cornbread and Poppy shivered. The shrub shivered.

"I like mice!" said the voice.

The shrub shivered.

Poppy grabbed a stone and stood up.

"I'll save you, Cornbread! Run!"

She threw the rock at the owl's toe.

48

"Ouch! Why'd you do that?" cried the owl.
"I like mice. Mice are my friends."

"We…we thought owls liked to eat mice?"
said Poppy.

"Not me," said the owl.
"I'm a vegetarian."

The large, fluffy, sniffling owl towered over them.

"I'm Bernard," he said.

"I'm sorry, Bernard....I'm Cornbread."

"I'm sorry, Bernard....I'm Poppy."

"What are you doing in the mountain?" asked Bernard. "I don't often see mice up here."

"We were looking for food," said Cornbread.

51

"I know a place with food. Lots of it!" said
Bernard.

Cornbread and Poppy liked the sound of that.

"Can you show us?" asked Poppy, collecting their wagon.

"I sure can! It's faster if you jump on!" said Bernard, offering them a ride.

And away they flew.

❄ The Food Problem ❄

A few moments later, they touched down at a small cabin. Smoke was puffing out of a chimney.

"This is my friend's house!" said Bernard.

The cabin door slowly creaked open. An
old mouse came out to greet them.

"Ms. Ruthie! You know Ms. Ruthie?" said
Bernard, Cornbread, and Poppy all at once.

"Cornbread! Poppy! Why, I haven't seen you two in ages!" said Ms. Ruthie. "Come inside and get warm!"

"G'bye, friends!" said Bernard, flapping his great big wings, lifting up and away into Holler Mountain.

"Ms. Ruthie, we thought you were…a goner," said Cornbread.

"I was a goner, all right. I'd gone and moved up here to the mountain. I like being alone!" said Ms. Ruthie. "I'm happy finally to have some mice to keep me company, though! What brings you up here anyway?"

They explained Poppy's food problem.

"Bernard seemed to think you had some food you could share?" asked Poppy sheepishly.

"Oh, do I!" said Ms. Ruthie.

"I've been saving for years! I'm the only mouse who forages up here on Holler Mountain. Take all you want!"

There were jars and jars of berry preserves.

Bags and bags of grain. Hunks and hunks
of cheese.

"But you have to have a cup of Ms. Ruthie's
tea before you go!" their friend said.

It was getting late. Ms. Ruthie helped
Cornbread and Poppy load up the food.
She even gave them a canister of her
special tea leaves to go.

Then she fastened snow skis to their feet
and to their wagon for a speedy journey
home.

"Thank you so much, Ms. Ruthie!" said Poppy. "You're a real lifesaver! What can I ever do to make it up to you?"

"Just come back and visit sometime!" said Ms. Ruthie.

Cornbread and Poppy
zipped back down the
mountain on the skis.

Naturally, Poppy loved it.

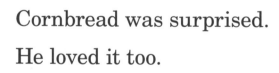

Cornbread was surprised.
He loved it too.

It was quite an adventure.

At Poppy's house, they unloaded and put away all the food.

The snow was very deep. Cornbread helped Poppy shovel her walkway.

They had a cup of Ms. Ruthie's tea to reward themselves for a job well done.

"To old friends," said Poppy.

"Let's ski some more!" said Cornbread.

"Shouldn't we shovel the walkway at your
house, Cornbread? It's almost dark."

"Nah, I'll do it later!" he said.